Serve the People

Serve the People

CHARLIE LEHMAN

RESOURCE *Publications* • Eugene, Oregon

SERVE THE PEOPLE

Resource Publications
An Imprint of Wipf and Stock Publishers
199 W. 8th Ave., Suite 3
Eugene, OR 97401

www.wipfandstock.com

PAPERBACK ISBN: 978-1-7252-6503-5
HARDCOVER ISBN: 978-1-7252-6504-2
EBOOK ISBN: 978-1-7252-6505-9

Manufactured in the U.S.A.   04/29/20

To Lorraine, the beautiful nurse who read my story and married and stayed with me in spite of that.

ACKNOWLEDGMENTS

GOD BLESSED ME WITH the experiences and milieu for this short work of fiction, and with indispensable help from the following people. Without the prodding and encouragement of the writers' workshop led by Father Jack Sparks of blessed memory, I would not have finished my story. Without the influence and encouragement of Berkeley Street Theatre comrade Jeanne DeFazio and Dr. William Spencer, it would have sat in the last of a series of drawers. Deacon Rick Billings made it an acceptable manuscript. Lawyer, LA Co. Public Defender paralegal extraordinaire', mentor, and steadfast friend Mara Dale Link committed to anything needed for publication. Project Manager Matt Wimer gave this untested author a shot.

"I AM SICK OF your jive." The accuser was a squat white kid in his mid-twenties. His dirty, shoulder-length hair was kept off his face by an orange bandana. Over his paisley—one sleeve ended at the elbow—shirt he wore a stained denim jacket with an off-white, *faux* sheepskin lining; straight black jeans; and orange sneakers. He wanted money.

"Can't we talk about this alone?" She was thirty years old, as short and stocky as the kid to whom she spoke, and even more pale. Her short red hair had come out of the rollers one hour ago. She wore a modest beige blouse, a dark blue car coat, light blue slacks, and practical brown shoes.

"Uh-uh. No more 'alone.' You said you'd give me my money tonight, and I want it." His greater volume emphasized the rejection of privacy.

The hallway of Durant House in Berkeley was not private. Ten feet away, three young men sat on three couches, their sleeping bags marking their shares of the floor of the large living room. At the door, seven feet away, a barrel-chested Hawaiian explained to two young women from New Jersey that Durant House was full and offered alternatives for the night. The women argued that they had stayed the night before and been promised another night. The pay phone four feet from the woman in the car coat and the boy in the orange sneakers rang for the eighth time. As a Durant House member, the kid in the orange sneakers had some responsibility to answer it. But this time the two Durant House members in the kitchen talking about God could interrupt their conversation to pick up the phone. Martin Luther Klein's face tightened. Tonight there would be a couple differences in the otherwise routine night at Durant House. He would not answer the phone. He would not overlook the slightly slurred speech of Monica Neal. He would not listen to her explanation. Filial love and faith in this sister had been replaced by suspicion and faith in his suspicion. No more believing in spite of what he saw and heard.

"Marty, can't you be patient with me? C'mon, let's go outside. This is just between you and I. You're a good brother. I think we ought to pray about this."

"No. You gonna give me my money, or you gonna jive your way out of it?"

"Good-by, Marty. I'll talk to you next week."

Monica pushed past the two skinny girls from New Jersey, walked half a block, and got into a drug dealer's GTO.

Five minutes later the women from New Jersey were gone. The boy in the orange sneakers was drinking coffee in the hallway. The big Hawaiian came over to him and asked: "Monica gone? She had some money, you know. She paid me fifty bucks of her back rent. I can't believe how much she owes you. She gonna come back next weekend?"

"Yeah," said Marty. She didn't come back, though. Marty never saw her again. That was the most he expected.

1

MARTY KLEIN KNOCKED FOUR times on the door of the pink stucco house. He was frustrated. He had failed to find Mary Briggs teaching fourth grade. In the last eight minutes he had walked away defeated twice from the unanswered door. The drought had not done the "lawn," gray bushes, or dusty porch any good. Marty sweated and rubbed his right eye. When it rained, plants thrived and shot voluminous patterns of pollen. During the drought there was no rain to clear the air of the pollen shot out by the thirsty, leafy pests. Marty wished the grasses, trees, weeds, and flowers dead. The door opened inward, and a lady in her seventies blinked at the short white boy. "Yes?" she asked.

"Mary Briggs?" Klein asked.

"She's sick."

"I gotta see her."

"I'm her aunt."

"I gotta see her."

Mary Briggs walked into the living room. She took short, unsteady steps. She stood in a yellow bathrobe, tall and thin. She had a diamond stud in her nose. She was forty years old.

"Mary Briggs?"

"Yes."

"I have some legal papers for you."

Terry Marcos sat in a beanbag chair in his living room and squinted over the sights of his pistol. Ignoring the rerun of

Emergency, he fired plastic pellets through the open door into the mobile of beer cans and hangers. He heard loud knocking on his door. He walked over and spoke through the closed door: "Who is it?"

"Terry Marcos?" Then poorly stifled laughter. Terry opened the door. Marty grinned over two six-packs of Budweiser. "Terry Marcos, I have some legal papers for you." Terry gave a little shriek, feinted with each hand, and aimed a kick at Marty's jaw. Marty blocked it with the top six-pack, which fell to the carpet. The guys pulled out two beers and put the rest away.

"Yeah, man, I knew I could do it. I really feel alive. My first serve. This is it!"

"A poor, sick, old school teacher. I'll bet you feel like a big man."

"Patty! I gotta call Patty! She got me the interview. She created a monster!"

An Alameda County court clerk, Patty had told Marty of Oakland's top attorney service's need of a process server in Berkeley. Rick at the Morden Attorney Service had been impressed with Marty's four years of Berkeley residence and his preparation: he'd read the California process server's manual before applying.

Holding his cold fourth beer to his forehead, Marty threw his empty third can into Terry's crotch. "Hey! Pay attention! This is a big day for me. Forget the call. I'll see Patty next week. Wow, I can hardly believe it. I'm a process server! I'm still scared, man, but I did it. I'm gonna be good." Marty laughed and grinned and looked his roommate in the eye. He rarely looked people in the eye. Terry laughed along and shook his head and smiled back.

2

ON THE THIRD MONDAY morning Rick Jensen was pleased. "You're doin' all right, *amigo*. You keep this up, you got nothin' to worry about. OK, no rush on the two Summons and Complaints you got there, but only two more Berkeley papers for you, one subpoena and one small claims. How about a couple Oakland?"

Marty looked at the addresses typed on the yellow office forms, clipped to the legal papers. Some of the addresses were unfamiliar. The others were recognizable, but ghetto. "Uh, no thanks. I'm not an ex-Marine or a karate freak." He was usually polite—especially where authority, power, or fear was involved, and he didn't want to be put in jeopardy for three bucks a paper. Marty had an ingratiating, non-threatening manner. He was starting to realize that this, along with his young and harmless looks, made him a good process server.

Rick's brown eyes sparkled mischievously behind his photogray aviator glasses, and the right horn of his moustache turned down when he laughed. "OK, man, just make an attempt on your way back to Berkeley. It's right off Telegraph Avenue. Shouldn't be too hard. It's a hot one. Guy wants his old lady served. He called twice since Wednesday. Our Cecil or Cecilia or whatever he, she, or it calls itself says he tried it Friday or Saturday, but that doesn't mean much. Cecil's a flake. So the guy says his old lady'll be home 'til noon today. It's a rush, so it's a four-dollar serve. Serve that *chiquita*. Then call me."

Ellen Morden leaned against the doorway of her office, took a drag off her Kool, and frowned. She disapproved of Rick's insulting of Cecil, the only transsexual at the Morden Attorney Service. It wasn't that she liked Cecil/Cecilia's work or that she advocated for this server's choice. Ellen considered it unnecessarily cruel to mock someone out of the sexual mainstream. She called, "Marty, you through there? Can you come in here a minute?"

Ellen usually spoke quickly, and with economy. She ran an attorney service—getting information, fielding complaints, and giving orders—under pressure from her clients, from the top law firms to the ranting spouses. She was forty-two years old, short and petite. Her hair was expensively styled, dyed blonde, and sprayed. Her clothes fit her station in life. She could talk as tough as anyone in Oakland, and her laugh was as nuts as Marty's.

Marty replied: "Yeah, sure, Ellen. That it, Rick?"

Marty had never been in the boss's office or had had a conversation with her. Ellen began: "Don't be afraid. Sit down. I want to talk to you about Saturday. What happened on the Purple serve?"

The Purple was a boutique in downtown Berkeley. The attorney service had been hired to serve the business with a subpoena for records, and Marty was the Berkeley server. He had made the Purple serve on his eleventh day as a process server.

"Well, I made two attempts to serve the paper at the Purple. Each time the manager told me the owner wasn't in, that he was expected back in fifteen minutes. I got sick of wasting my time and gas going back there, so I tried to serve the manager. She wouldn't sign the proof of service, wouldn't take the paper, but she gave me the owner's home address. She told me I might upset him if I bothered him at home, and I thought, 'Well, we can't upset this important man. We can jive Marty around and have him waste his money and gas on a three-dollar serve.' So I drove out to his home in the Berkeley hills.

"I tried to serve the owner of the Purple boutique at his home, but he didn't want to sign the paper. He's Pakistani or something, about 35, successful-looking, and I guess he was unfamiliar with civil law and a little scared. I explained that he had to take the subpoena and the witness fee check, that it was probably a request for records and a witness fee, and that he might get paid for his mileage, too. He said he wouldn't take it or sign the slip. He had an American friend there—older, portly. His friend said he'd have to take the subpoena, but didn't have to sign anything. So our guy said he wouldn't take anything until his lawyer called him back and explained everything. I told him he had to accept it, and he told me to get in my car and get out , or he'd beat me up and, he pushed me a little. I threw the subpoena and the check on his front walk, behind the gate. He threw them out on the sidewalk as I walked away."

"Rick," Ellen called, "Rick, come in here a minute."

"Yes, ma'am."

"Rick, we gotta do this Purple serve over at the business address. There's still plenty of time on it. Give it to . . . "

Marty watched a spiny black and white zebra-striped fish as Ellen re-assigned the serve, and he worried. There were eight-foot fish tanks on either side of Ellen's desk, one next to the glass partition that separated her office from the rest of the business and one next to the view of Oakland's Lake Merritt from the tenth floor of the building.

Ellen finished her instructions to Rick and addressed Marty: "You did a good job, honey. You came across a new situation and did the best according to what you'd been told, and you got it served. You didn't have to get a signature, but you didn't know that. We'll have to serve it over at the business address, but that's OK. You'll get paid anyhow. You like the fish? That spiny one's a real doll, real friendly. Can't touch him, though. He's poisonous." The phone rang. "Gotta go, honey. You, too. Go back to Berkeley and do your thing. By-by."

3

DURING THE NEXT WEEKS Marty's status as the Berkeley server was solidified. He made deliveries and pick-ups at attorneys' offices. He bought tropical fish food at two stores in downtown Oakland and one in Berkeley. He picked up Ellen's Valium. He had the office postage machine reloaded at the post office. He brought legal papers to court clerks for filing and to judges for signing.

And he served lots and lots of legal papers. The one who pays for the service is the client. There is no word in the process server's jargon for the one who gets the paper. He served all kinds: the rich, the poor, business, and government. Some serves were satisfying, and some were frustrating. On several serves he returned again and again (made "attempt" after "attempt") to empty houses or found that the would-be recipient no longer lived, or had never lived, at that address. He did not complete the serve on these, so he was not paid for them. He became accustomed to bringing disagreeable news. Within the first month he no longer prayed before entering each home or office.

One May morning, a little over a month into his new career, Marty reported to the Morden office, picked up more papers, pulled his filthy white Camaro out of the downtown lot, and drove to a shopping center in Oakland. This was to be an easy, routine matter: a subpoena for records of a doctor's office. But the address in the office tower atop the Oakland shopping center was that of a "receiver" for the doctor. He parked in the lot on top of the shopping center, rode up in the elevator, and knocked on the door.

"Come in," said Molly Suzuki. No one would ever be struck as hard by the woman behind the desk in the small office as this process server. Short and full-bodied, she had wide cheeks and dark skin. Her black hair was cut in a long shag. She wore a Mexican blouse with puffy, short sleeves—white, with orange stitching. Her eyes were warm, and she smiled at Marty. Her voice was soft and full of energy. "Hi. Can I help you?"

"Uh, yeah. Oh, yeah." The receptionist noticed his attention and smiled back. "Hi. Uh, I have some legal papers for Dr. Gordon."

"OK. I can take them."

"OK. Would you sign my receipt, please?"

"Uh-huh." Molly took the subpoena and signed the receipt. "Here you go." She smiled at him again.

"Yeah, thanks. I'll see you." Marty turned away.

"Have a nice day," said Molly.

Marty stole one more quick look.

Back in his car, Marty filled out the paperwork. He never ran across people this friendly. He made a note of the encounter.

That night Terry Marcos let Marty have it: "Stick to your own kind, white boy."

"Booo. She's really sweet. I told her, 'Zis iss Leutnant Klein uff State Security. Here are your legal papers, gookchen. You vill report to zuh kamp at Santa Rita on June One at seven AM. Iff you haff any quveshtions, hesitate to call my off-iss.' She loved it. A model servee."

"You're sick, Klein. You should have worked for the Gestapo. Maybe the DEA will take you."

"I haff my prin-zipples. I vill nut verk for zuh Drug Enforcement Administration. Besides, my eyes are too weak, and I signed too much stuff against the war."

One week later Marty returned to the rooftop parking lot. He had felt self-conscious the first time he'd spoken to Molly Suzuki. He had not showered or shaved that morning. The process server sweated as he worked in the warmth of the drought and the air pollution of the East Bay, and especially in his car. On this morning he showered, shaved, and applied lime aftershave. Marty sighed, prayed, "Help," knocked twice on the door, stuck his head in, and smiled at the receptionist.

She smiled back warmly. "Hi. Do you have another paper?"

Marty leaned against the door frame and turned towards her. "Uh, no, uh, I wanted to see if you'd like to, uh, have lunch with me. We could go to one of the places downstairs." The mall's food court had Mexican, Chinese, German, ice cream . . .

"Well, I don't eat lunch. I'm trying to lose weight."

"Oh. OK, well. . ."

"Wait, it's twelve now, and I get my lunch break in half an hour. I usually get a yogurt at the market downstairs. Could you come back in half an hour?"

"Sure. I'll buy you a cup of yogurt."

Half an hour later Marty was back. Molly got up and opened the door to the inner office. She told her boss, a 45-year-old graying man in his shirtsleeves, that she was going to lunch, picked up her olive drab shoulder bag, and led Marty to the elevator. Marty bought her a cup of yogurt and himself a blueberry cheesecake shake. They sat down in the central area of the food court.

Marty gulped a mouthful of shake and asked her, "What do you do up there? Accept service all day?"

Molly sighed. "I do that, and I answer the phone, and I push papers around. Mr. Cooper checks everything I do at least twice." She sighed again and looked into her yogurt. Marty took this opportunity to stare. Today she was wearing a pre-washed blue denim jump suit. "How did you become a process server?"

"I read an article in the paper about process servers. A friend works at the county courthouse, and she told me about an opening at the Morden office." They talked about favorite movies for fifteen minutes, and Marty asked, "What did you major in?"

"Psychology," she answered. "I have a gift for counseling. Someday I may get my master's and get certified, but I don't know how I'd be any more use to the Lord and people with it. Oh, gee, I gotta get back to work."

Marty accompanied her to the elevator. "Hey, can I buy you a real lunch on Friday?"

"No, Marty. I want you to be my guest next time. I want you to meet my community. I live in a Christian house, and we try to help people. Can you come over for dinner on Friday? It's on Durant, in Berkeley."

4

Friday night Marty Klein came to dinner showered, shampooed, shaven, and lime-aftershaven. He'd asked Molly not to reveal his identity to the Durant House members. On this Friday only three of the house members were present: Freddy, the barrel-chested Hawaiian who had been the head of the house when Marty had lived there; John, a veteran of the Madison anti-war movement; and Molly.

Also present were two "crashers," those allowed to stay one to three days: Rattler, from Boston; and Dave, from New York City. Rattler was eighteen years old. He had hitchhiked across the country, and he reveled in this achievement, along with his cozy relationship with a Berkeley cop. He had a life-sized tattoo of a rattlesnake. Its fangs whipped out on the back of his right hand. It ran up his arm, looped around his neck, and ran down his left arm, its rattles on the left middle finger, ending at the nail. Rattler talked nonstop. Dave was twenty-seven years old. He had shoulder-length, greasy, blonde hair and a stubble beard. He wore a US Army field jacket, zipped up to his Adam's apple. Dave shivered from time to time, softly answered questions from Freddy and Molly, and volunteered nothing.

They all dined on Freddy's excellent sweet and sour pork and rice. Freddy asked Marty, "Why'd you leave the community, dude?"

Marty was ready: "People didn't really want the Good News. Now I bring them the bad news." Only Molly laughed.

At the end of the meal Marty asked Molly if she'd like to have a beer at Pik's, a beer and pizza joint at the center of the Berkeley circus, three blocks from the Christian boarding house. The sidewalks were crowded with university students. Marty and Molly were asked by a twenty-year-old alcoholic and a forty-year-old alcoholic, at different corners, for spare change. Molly stopped to talk with the first one—she knew him—but Marty glared at her, and she moved on. Molly smiled and shrugged at the older bum on the next block. Marty looked him right in the eye and shook his head. The process server and the receptionist ascended the stairs to Pik's, opened the door, and were blasted by the juke box, laughter, loud voices, and cigarette smoke. Friday night—mostly University of California students; and some derelicts, working people, Jesus freaks, and petty criminals filled the place. Thirteen sat or stood at the bar. Three danced at the juke box near the toilets. The rest ate, drank, talked, or played dominoes at tables lined up or spaced individually. Marty and Molly were lucky to get a table. Marty ordered a pitcher of beer from the bar and pointed to the table where Molly sat. The pitcher and two mugs came, and the two talked about current movies.

"Marty, why did you leave the community?"

"I'm a Lutheran. I've always been a Lutheran, ever since Lutheran Child Welfare got me parents, and they got me baptized. I go to church on Sunday, confess my sins, hear the word of God, take Communion, and sing to God without being a half-assed pseudo-social worker or a target for every loser, wacko, or hustler who hitchhikes through Berkeley. I've had it with 'community.'"

"That's not the attitude Jesus would have, Marty."

"I'm not Jesus. That's the best attitude I can come up with." Marty looked at the beer signs over the bar and decided it was time for some Ballantine Ale. Molly touched one of the hands supporting Marty's chin. He said: "Oh, I'm sorry. It's not your fault. You've been nicer to me than, than . . ." He picked her hand off the table and held it to his lips. Molly put her free hand on Marty's. "Now I can't drink," said Marty.

Molly laughed and bobbed her head. "Uh-uh. Talk to me. Living at Durant House isn't that bad. Come on. What have you got against community?"

He kissed her fingers and said: "OK, sure. But I want another beer." He had seen the Austrian waitress, out of place in a toilet like Pik's. He waved and shouted, "S'cuse me!" over *Brown Sugar*. "You got Ballantine Ale?"

Marty began, "I was involved with an ex-junkie—ha—for about a year. She wasn't the first, but she was the worst. At Durant House, you'd just help anyone with his problem, her problem. I took her to the ER after she got beat up. I picked her up at the Berkeley Free Clinic after she cut her wrists. I pulled her back into my car when she tried to jump out on the freeway. She didn't try very hard. I gave her a ride into Oakland—turned out to be a heroin deal, right there on the street. I saw it in my rearview mirror. I didn't want her getting hurt, so I didn't leave her there. After listening to me for a couple months, she accepted Christ. The big day came: she was baptized by Pastor Deirdre. I cried. We kept helping her with her crises and her day-to-day stuff. We ate together, had some laughs, and went to the movies. Nothing romantic. We put her on a plane to Detroit to get her kid, and she brought him back. I lent her money for an apartment in the suburbs. I lent her money for an attorney, when they tried to take her kid away. I wouldn't listen when people like her landlord and the attorney tried to talk to me alone about her. *No*—Monica was a baptized member of our *community*. She was one of us, one of me. Well, she wasn't so 'ex,' I found out later. I confronted her, and we had a 'dialogue,' and I left the community."

5

If the server were lucky, he would be given a description of the person to be served, along with the person's home and business addresses. The first of these was often missing, and so was one of the other two. The description of Jackie Bannon was accurate: five foot, eight inches tall; 200 pounds, black. In person he looked a little chubby, but muscular, a little like Joe Frazier. He had a short natural haircut, and his beard was better than Frazier's. Mr. Bannon had a gold tooth (front, upper), the name "Mona" tattooed on his left chest, and a scar across his nose. This information, except for the muscles and the comparison to the former World Heavyweight Champion, was on the yellow sheet clipped to the small claims paper Marty Klein was to present Jackie Bannon. Descriptions of Jackie's yellow Camaro and blue Mercedes-Benz were also on the yellow sheet. Twice Marty would be given a photo of the person he was to serve. Outside of these instances, he was never given a description better than the description of Jackie Bannon.

The client on this serve was Max Konig, who ran a finance company called Easy Money. Its office was next door to the Elaine Morden Attorney Service. Konig was a bald six-footer who wore wire-rim spectacles like Marty's. He looked like an out-of-shape Mr. Clean in a leisure suit. Max spoke loudly and quickly, with an insistent whine. His three slender, pallid office assistants wore heavy make-up, black dresses, and high heels. Their black hair was perfect. Marty noticed that they managed to come to work during daylight hours, but he never wanted to find himself alone with any of them. Marty had done a few jobs for Max Konig, independent of his work as a process server. It was like a serve, but you only had to remind the Easy Money customer to call Mr. Konig today, see Mr. Konig today, or make the overdue payment—*today*. If the client were out, Marty would leave a note. In this way, it was more profitable than serving papers, because you got paid whether or not you found the person in. Marty didn't mind serving papers to poor or minority people. But as Konig's collector , he found himself hassling only poor blacks, and he didn't like that. After five jobs, Konig and Klein got sick of each other.

On this afternoon in late June, Marty was bringing a summons to appear in small claims court to Easy Money customer Jackie Bannon. He saw the address and the parked Mercedes and Camaro and parked half a block down, on the Berkeley/Oakland border street. He usually parked around the corner. He didn't want the people he was serving to associate hassles or "pigs" with his white Camaro and smash his windshield or wait for him in a parking lot—now or later. And he didn't want the *cops* he served to remember his car, either. After a couple hundred serves, Berkeley could seem like a small town, and it would get worse.

Marty walked up the steps, crossed the porch, and knocked on the screen door. The steps, porch, and door were of old, dusty wood, blue-gray paint flaking off them for years. Marty knocked gently on the screen door, and a man fitting Jackie Bannon's description appeared, dressed only in cut-off jeans. "Yes?" he asked Marty through the screen door.

"Hi. Jackie Bannon?"

"Yes," the man answered.

"I have some legal papers for you."

"He's not here. I'm watching his house. If you want me to take something for him, I can give it to him when he comes back."

The guy looked just like the description, and he had responded to the name. Or had Marty misunderstood him? He had to serve the right person, and he wasn't sure of the guy's identity now. This man was even willing to take the paper, but he said he wasn't Jackie Bannon. Under these circumstances, Marty couldn't let him take the small claims summons for another person (called "sub-serving," and allowed under some circumstances). So Marty told him, "No. That's OK. See ya."

Marty walked around the corner to a pay phone outside a donut shop and called the Morden office. "Hi, Rick. This is Marty. Listen, I got a guy out here that fits Jackie Bannon's description right down to the gold tooth and the tattoo, but he won't cop to the name."

"Just a second, *amigo*." Marty waited, sweating, worrying, looking at rows of sugary donuts and watching a couple teenagers eat theirs. Rick came back on. "Yeah, man. That's him. Serve that sucker." Marty had been afraid of that. He wasn't going to stand on that crummy porch in a black neighborhood on this stifling afternoon and call Joe Frazier's long-lost identical twin a liar.

Back on the porch, Marty knocked again. The same man appeared and asked, "Yeah? What you want now?"

Marty smiled and said,"Y'know, you can help me out. I checked, and you can take the paper for him."

"Oh, no. I ain't takin' no paper. And don't leave nothin' on my friend's porch, neither."

Rats, thought Marty, he knows about drop serves. In a "drop serve" the person refuses to take the paper. So the server just tells him that the legal papers are his, drops them in front of him, and walks away. It's legal as long as the recipient knows the general nature ("legal papers") of what he's getting and the server is within "reasonable distance" of the recipient.

"Come on, man. It's no big deal. It's just a small claims paper. Just give it to him when you see him again."

"Uh-uh. You get outta here. Don't you leave nothin' on this porch, neither. I'm not cleanin' up this porch after you." The guy picked up a bamboo stick and began slapping his hand with it. "You drop anything on this porch, and I'm gonna make you pick it up."

Marty responded, "Are you gonna hit me over a lousy small claims paper?"

"I'm not gonna hit you. I'm gonna make you pick it up." The larger man was also sweating. "And I'm sick 'a talkin' with you." Jackie Bannon's volume rose: "You get offa my friend's porch. I'm gonna get my Dobie. Honey," he called back into the house, "bring

17

the dog and the collar out here. I see two of my brothers 'cross the street. You better get off my friend's porch."

Marty thought the threats about the Doberman and the guy's buddies were jive, but he didn't want to stick around and find out. He didn't think things were going to get any better, so he said, "OK, here's your paper," and dropped it at the bottom of the screen door. He turned and walked off the porch. Before he reached the sidewalk, Jackie Bannon grabbed him.

Terry Marcos had poured the oil and thrown the finely-chopped broccoli into the wok. He then threw in some crumbly tofu and the snow peas he loved. He was slicing the pork into little bits when he heard Marty's key in the lock. When he heard the door open, he yelled over Boz Scaggs, "Hey, dude, you want some food?" Terry accepted a sixteen-ounce beer from Marty as he came in to look at the food. "I ought to teach you how to cook this stuff for your new friend. What's up? Did you evict a paraplegic?"

Marty told Terry about the Jackie Bannon attempted serve. "I took the paper back. I'm not stopping the flow of heroin into Oakland. I'm helping some legitimate creep who's two steps above a loan shark screw some deadbeat. And I wasn't going to fight Joe Frazier over a three-dollar serve. He coulda' broken my jaw! He coulda' killed me! He had seventy-five pounds on me!" Marty yelled over the record and the sizzling food. "Rick and Ellen said it was OK, and they got mad at Konig for giving us a paper on a known animal like Bannon. That's what they said to me, anyway. And they're going to pay me my three bucks anyhow, even though I didn't get it served. Whoopee. I'm twenty-six, not sixteen. I don't need this. This bastard lies to me and pushes me around and threatens me, and I take the paper back. And *I* feel cheap. *He* probably feels great. It's a good thing I got a sense of humor about all this," said Marty, opening his second half-quart. "You know, it's true. Your throat does get dry when you're scared."

6

MARTY GAVE THE TOLL-TAKER seventy-five cents and returned his smile. He hit the gas and smiled at his ability to get a chirp out of the tires with only a 283. He had been lucky or fortunate or blessed or whatever to get a car with a fairly small engine with some punch. A friend had traded up to a Z/28 and given Marty a deal on the white Camaro. Karl had spent an hour on the maintenance of the car every Sunday and changed the oil twice as often as required. Marty would have enjoyed a street machine, but he was too practical to pay the price and too lazy to maintain one. He kept up the maintenance on his cheap pseudo-sports car, but not its appearance. The Camaro wore eighteen months of dirt, the carpets were ripped, the armrests and glove compartment door were gone, and the passenger seat slid forward with Molly whenever Marty came to a stop.

Marty's face was tense with concentration behind the round, black-lensed glasses that made him look like Jefferson Airplane's bassist. He quickly checked the traffic on either side as he beat the other cars out of the toll booths, overtook a Skylark, and made it into the second lane from the left, just at the point where the Dunbarton Bridge started over the Bay. Marty checked the speed, looked in his review mirror, and slowed down twenty miles per hour, to the limit. He smiled a tight smile, listened to the music, and watched the water.

The instrumental introduction about the Kent/Cambodia protest deaths boomed out of the three speakers. Goose bumps ran along Marty's neck, shoulders, and arms, and he clenched his teeth.

The first couple miles of the bridge stretched in a flat trajectory fifteen feet above what appeared to Marty to be a cross between the Great Salt Lake and the Mekong Delta. He had seen the Great Salt Lake. He had seen the war on TV. Marty loved this bridge. It went on and on over the tan, gray, white, and pink sand or minerals and the swamp that looked like a rice paddy. It was unlike any bridge over which he had driven. The high-quality, emotion-laden music added to the experience.

When the song finished, Marty spoke to Molly, still watching the swamp: "When I was in college, I had no sympathy for them. Funny, my Dad voted for Nixon three times, but he wrote him and objected to the invasion of a neutral country. Not me—the gooks didn't fight fair, so why should we? The students? They asked for it. But I always loved that song, that and the Jefferson Airplane anti-war stuff."

Molly looked up from the summons she'd been reading. "Uh-huh. I'm really interested in this lawsuit. The people you're going to serve are being sued for an accident in the Co-op parking lot . . . "

"Hold it," Marty said, "I don't want to hear about it."

"But . . . "

"Hey, my job is to slap Dr. and Mrs. Randall with these summonses. Maybe they did something wrong or negligent, and they'll have to pay for it. But maybe they're real nice people, living saints. Maybe they make Mother Theresa look like a decadent opportunist. Maybe they did nothing wrong, and the guy who hired some attorney, who hired Ellen, who's paying me is a slimy, lying bastard who's victimizing the poor Randalls. I know how it is. I don't care. If they ask me anything, I gotta be able to say, 'I don't know about it. I just deliver the papers.'"

"How can you do that? How can you participate in that?"

Molly wasn't angry, so Marty allowed himself a chuckle. "It's my thing. It's what I do best, who I am."

"Don't you care about them?"

"I don't involve myself in people's lives. I'm no good at that. I'm not going to save anybody."

"What do you mean? 'It's who I am. I'm not going to save any-body.' You're a Christian, Marty, a new creature. There's no limit to what you can do through Christ."

"Gee, I guess there's nobody I can't reach, I can't serve. Brando! Nixon!"

"Come on, Marty!"

"Yeah, well, it doesn't work out that way. Listen, I treat people with respect. I serve people the way I would like to be served. I'm polite."

"You're cold. You're detached, unloving. I don't like that. You're so much better than that."

"No, I'm *not*. If you can bleed for the losers and do some good, fine. Just don't bleed out, as the ambulance guys say. You're on my little list of very special people, the people I refuse to call 'community.' Ellen, for example. She needs me." Molly sighed and looked at him. She touched his lips with her fingers, and he smiled and took her hand.

After driving another thirty minutes, Marty found the Randalls at their suburban home. The circular drive and hedge formed a mini-cul-de-sac. Marty left the Camaro across the only opening, smiled at Molly, and said, "Don't let anybody out."

Marty switched his junkie shades for his John Lennon wire rims before approaching the tall lady weeding at the front of the house. He didn't want to simulate a Manson Attack. "Excuse me, is Dr. Randall free?"

"Yes, he's inside. Are you in his poetry class?"

"No, it's just a little business. I won't be long."

Mrs. Randall called her husband into the front yard, and Marty served them both. They were gracious. They were cultured, success-ful people. They wouldn't think of ugliness directed at a young man for making a legal delivery. Threaten him? Grab him? Drag him behind the hot tub and break his kneecaps? Those behaviors are out of the question for Berkeley professors and Junior League sustain-ing members. These responses are not only breaches of etiquette. They are violations of the law, possibly subjecting violators to arrest, shackling, strip-searching, big legal bills, and media coverage. Stuff like that happens to other people.

Yes, Marty would rather work tall professors than tattooed jailbirds. Successful people disdained ugliness, and they had a lot more to lose. The Randalls only did one unpleasant thing to Marty, involuntarily. They'd believed him to be an undergraduate and were ready to help him with his assignment. Mrs. Randall had an MA in English, and she enjoyed talking with students. When he had handed them the papers, the hurt had shown in their eyes. Marty had looked away and mumbled, "I have to go. Good-by." Shame had warmed his face as he walked to the Camaro.

Molly had watched the encounter from the car, quite interested. She stopped talking when she noticed the change in Marty.

Marty concluded that every job had its distasteful duties, and that he was lucky that he didn't have to do something even more unpleasant. These things would happen sometimes, and he would feel bad about it for awhile. He'd get used to it. Maybe he shouldn't. *So what.* This was a determination, not a question. He had done a good job and would make a little more money on this high-priced rush serve. He would charge thirty-five dollars for each of the two serves, based on his time, the mileage, and the urgency. And he had had a beautiful day with a wonderful woman. "And I even feel a little sorry for those people," he thought, "which means I'm a pretty nice guy—for a crud." He laughed out loud, and Molly turned, glad to see him out of his mood.

7

AFTER MARTY DROPPED MOLLY at Durant House, he served a couple more papers in Berkeley, the last one in the black neighborhood. When he'd moved to California and seen it, he'd responded: "Ghetto? This is a nice neighborhood."

Klein drove past his last servee's house and parallel-parked around the corner. As he walked toward the house, a Berkeley Police car passed him, and the cop focused on him.

Having served the slight, twenty-year-old woman, Marty returned to his car. The same cop—big black guy with a shaved head and a full, droopy moustache—was double-parked two car-lengths back. The Berkeley Police Department was pretty good about letting their men grow their hair and beards. As Marty approached his Camaro, he and the cop made eye contact, each one curious and a bit assertive. Marty climbed into the back seat of his car, extended his legs out between the front seats, turned on the radio, and took his time doing the paperwork on the serve. He focused the rearview mirror on the cop and checked it repeatedly. The cop's focus stayed on Marty.

The process server squeezed into the driver's seat, readjusted the mirror, started up the car, and drove towards home. The cop stayed with him, close enough to turn pedestrians' heads in a business district. Marty kept the car at the posted 25 miles per hour, thinking this was probably annoying to other drivers. They picked up a second unit, which fell in behind the first and followed them out of the black neighborhood. A couple blocks from Marty's neighborhood, both cops hit the lights. Marty turned off a busy street and pulled to the curb. The cops double-parked in tandem behind the white Camaro.

Marty slowly opened the door with both hands and stepped out. The black cop directed him to raise his hands and frisked him. Officer Bruce Bernstein, the cop in the second car, also stepped forward, smiled, and asked, "You got a driver's license?" Marty recognized the blonde cop with the goatee and guessed that Officer Bernstein recognized him.

One month before Marty had served Bruce Bernstein in the Berkeley Police station. He didn't like making personal serves there. Cops covered for each other. A server could wait an hour or two for someone to come in from patrol, only to have the guy warned off and be told he had gone home. It had to be done this way, because police officers' home addresses were confidential. Marty understood.

Officer Bernstein had not been warned off. He'd been told someone wanted to see him at the front desk. Marty served him with a small claims paper from a tire shop. Marty had felt a little bad about serving him in front of his sergeant, because he'd heard from an ex-cop friend that police departments frown on officers' racking up bad debts.

The bearded cop read the license. "Martin Luther, huh? How's the Reformation going? How's the fortress?" He cuffed Marty's right hand to his own driver's door and searched the car. The black cop watched the suspect's face and asked, "You got a key for the trunk?" Marty knew they weren't supposed to search the car, but he thought it better not to object or make smart remarks. He had nothing to hide. He was a little afraid they might toss a joint into his car, but he thought they were more ethical than that. Bernstein hadn't gotten upset about getting served.

"Nothing," the black cop called to Bernstein.

Marty thought, "Have to smoke your own grass tonight, officers?" He concentrated on looking innocent.

As Officer Bernstein searched the engine compartment, Officer Donnell (Marty read the name tag.) asked, "What were you doing in that neighborhood?"

Officer Bernstein answered for the suspect. "I know what he was doing, in addition, maybe, to sticking up a grocery. He's a process server."

"That's right, Officer."

Officer Donnell chuckled. "I wouldn't do that."

Bernstein asked, "What's this can bolted to the inside of your fender for?"

"Rags. To check my oil."

The cop slammed the hood. "Uh-huh. Empty your pockets on the hood." As Marty did this, Officer Bernstein walked back to his car and talked on his radio. Returning to the Camaro, he said, "OK, Mr. Klein. Collect your stuff. We're going to drive the victim by, see what she thinks of you. Take off your glasses."

Marty couldn't recognize somebody six feet away or cross a busy street safely without his glasses, but he didn't want to make waves. He thought of telling the police he'd majored in theatre and offering to wave one of their guns at the victim, get into it, stick-em-up. He smirked, then tried to look like an altar boy.

A police car with a young woman in the back seat drove by. Officer Bernstein spoke into the small plastic speaker on his shoulder: "OK, Yamada. Around the block, one more time, pass us again, but slow down." The bearded cop went over to the trunk of his unit and popped the trunk. His partner turned away from Marty. Bernstein returned to the suspect, handed him a ski mask, black, with red rings around the holes for the eyes and mouth and a red tuft on the top. "Put this on, Klein. Victim said the guy was wearing a ski mask."

Marty thought: "What the fuck? How's she going to identify me? She's going to identify the mask! But I didn't do anything. I better cooperate." He put the mask on.

The two Berkeley cops couldn't hold it in any longer. They laughed until they cried. They looked up at Marty and started laughing all over again. The black cop got control of himself first:"Hey, man. Sorry, a little sorry, to chump you off. Bernstein was just breakin' your balls. We see so much. Everyone hates us." Officer Donnell caught the ski mask Marty tossed him. He unlocked the cuffs from Marty and the Camaro's driver's door and tossed them, and then the ski mask, back to his partner. Then he handed Marty his business card. "If you can't stay outta trouble, call me. One time. Go on, get outta here."

8

One week later Marty had refused to come to Durant House for breakfast, and Molly had refused to let Marty buy her breakfast again. So Marty had asked Terry to get out of the apartment so he could be alone with her on a Saturday morning.

"Won't you stay and have some breakfast. I brought plenty of eggs, Terry." The roommate smiled at them.

"Out. Get outta here. Go get some Alka-Seltzer and pineapple. Or keep drinking."

Molly covered Marty's mouth and tickled his ribs from behind. He threw a subpoena from the stack on top of the refrigerator at Terry, and it bounced off the door the roommate slammed on his way out.

Molly taught Marty to make a better omelet. Molly wanted to hear process serving adventures, but Marty quickly changed the subject.

"I wouldn't serve papers for this money if it was dangerous. Fear's a subjective, irrational thing. Most people are pretty stupid about the worst threat, right? What, I mean Whom, should they fear? God, right? Hell. Who fears God?

"I got really scared at the zoo a year ago. I love the snake house. I'm looking at this Gaboon viper, this ugly, bloated snake. You get bit by this guy, and you feel like you're slowly burning to death. And this kid next to me is tapping on the glass right in front of this snake. They've got signs forbidding this, but this kid wants a reaction from this sleepy snake. The snake house is mobbed, and I'm right next to this kid and his girlfriend.

"The first time this kid hits the glass, I flinch and say, 'Hey!' He pauses, looks down at me, and hits the glass a little harder with his senior ring. This guy is about a foot taller than me, fifty pounds heavier than me, about eight years younger than me, black. He looks like he's on the basketball team *and* the football team and has never smoked a cigarette in his life.

"The Gaboon viper doesn't wake up, so this guy moves on to the King Cobras next door. Now they're a nervous species, and they're wide awake, pressing the glass. So this dude takes his senior ring, which is about the size of my Clonex, and bangs on the glass right where one of the King Cobras is kissing it, and the glass shimmies. The snake flares its hood.

"And I say, 'Will you cool it, man?' I never talk that way with big black guys, but I'm more afraid of these snakes than I am of him. This guy tells me to shut my hole and cocks his hand to give the King Cobra another shock, and I've blocked his hand down into the rail in front of the glass and stomped on his instep, and I'm glancing at the bushmaster next to the King Cobras and heading for the grizzlies. I was looking over my shoulder the rest of the day, but I paid my money, and I was going to see the animals.

"Serving papers I never got in a fight or got hurt. I got in trouble a couple times, and I got a couple good stories."

"What's the best one?" Molly asked.

"I had a small claims paper for a guy who worked at this gas station on Sacramento Avenue. First time I went down there, he wasn't in. Second time another one of the gas jockeys told me he wasn't sure if the guy still worked there. A couple days later I was serving papers in the Berkeley Hills, and I run across a street that rings a bell. It's the guy's home address.

"And I think, 'How come this guy who works in this lousy gas station is livin' in this rich neighborhood?'

"So I go up to the door and this nice lady answers—polite, serious: 'Oh. That's my son. He doesn't live here. I don't know where he lives.'

"The only thing I tell her is that I tried to get a hold of him at work, and she says, kinda sad: 'He doesn't work there anymore. He's been laid off.'

"So that means it's impossible—no home address, no business address. How am I going to serve him? His mother says, 'I don't even have his phone number.' But *then* she says, 'But he'll be home Sunday for dinner, on Mother's Day.'"

Molly had to laugh. "Marty, you didn't!"

"Yeah. Heh-heh-heh. And he was a real sport about it, too. My Mother's Day serve even impressed Rick and Ellen. Ahh, people help me serve their children, their parents. . . . I'm just blessed with this innocent look, this charm."

Molly asked him again about violence.

"The time I came closest to getting hurt was when I served a guy who looked just like Joe Frazier . . . . "

When Marty finished the story, Molly took his hand, looked into his eyes, and said, "I don't want you doing things like that."

"Hey, I don't want me doing things like that either."

"I'm serious, Marty. If you won't stop taking stupid chances for your own sake, think of me. I care for you."

"It's OK. That's my very worst story. That doesn't happen."

"Would you consider doing something else, for my sake?"

"Yeah, sure. If it got as bad as you think. If I really got hurt, sure."

"I don't *want* you getting hurt." Molly remembered something. "Take off your shoes."

"What?"

"Come on, take off your shoes. See, Marty, there. Just beneath the little toe. You've got corns. That's why it hurts when you walk. I can see it, the way you walk. How long have your feet felt bad?"

"Oh, a year, a year and a half."

"Marty, can't you take care of yourself? We're going to the drug store and get you some stuff, and you'll feel better in a week of two. Oh, Marty, look at your other foot."

9

MARTY HAD SERVED THE manager of Key #3, a rock venue that often featured performers as prestigious as Jerry Garcia. It had been unpleasant, even more unpleasant than the first time he had served him. Donny (Marty had been unable to get a last name.) had tried to intimidate him into not serving Key #3. It hadn't worked.

Donny looked like a mean Joe Walsh or Jimmy Buffett. He was a little taller and heavier than Marty. At 35, he was starting on a beer belly, but he often had to hump chairs, amps, props, and kegs around, and he was more than up to it. Donny had nice blond hair that curled around his shoulders and a blond gunfighter's moustache on his lined, sunburned face. Marty wondered if he'd gotten the drawl from the South or from bikers. As manager, Marty figured, Donny would have to be enough of a man to deal with drunks and thieves, but enough of a businessman to avoid obvious crime. Marty hoped he was more of a businessman.

The bouncer had been present both times. He rode a big Harley and owned a massage parlor. He was Donny's gentle giant, all seven feet of him, a giant-sized, low-key Abbie Hoffman.

Now it was Sunday, and, with the exception of his Mother's Day Serve, Marty observed Sunday as a day of worship and rest. Berkeley has a wonderful variety of buildings and trees, homes, and businesses—a great place to wander and look. Near Berkeley High, Marty made a left onto Bancroft and walked towards the University of California campus. Donny and a younger white guy exited an apartment and almost bumped into Marty at the sidewalk. Donny's buddy wore a long-sleeved T-shirt promoting the release of the President of the Oakland chapter of the Hells Angels, currently in Folsom State Prison for selling heroin.

Donny smiled. "Look at this creep."

As they passed him, Marty shrugged and said, "Everybody's got to do something for a livin'."

Marty feared they might throw a bottle from their car. He walked on, not looking back. Donny pulled his black Roadrunner into the alley in front of Marty, and the guys got out.

Donny smiled again. "C'mere friend, I wanna talk to you." With his right hand he grabbed Marty's left arm and pulled him lightly towards the car.

Losing faith in his ability to jive his way out of getting his face kicked into the dumpster to the right of the Roadrunner, Marty reluctantly fell back on force, light force. "Don't make him mad," he thought. He threw a circular block with his left arm, putting the pressure painfully onto Donny's right thumb and forcing him to release the arm. "No, man. I'm scared-a-you."

"You better not come around again."

"I respect tough guys, but it's business, man. It's not personal." Marty walked in an arc, away from them and into the street.

Donny's friend joined in: "You come around with another subpoena, and we'll make it personal."

Marty turned from them and walked the short distance to the corner. He crossed Shattuck Avenue, a main street, against the light, dodged a 240-Z, and flipped off the driver who honked at him. His heart pounding and his mouth dry, he refused to look back. He would hear them if they ran up behind him, and they would not drive across one of Berkeley's busiest streets against the light. Marty turned onto Bancroft and walked against traffic on this one-way street. Two steps beyond Shattuck Avenue, he looked back. They were gone.

Back at the apartment, Terry lapped up the story. When Marty repeated, "I'm scared-a-you," Terry laughed, and Marty gave the standard guys' response.

Marty paced back and forth, clenched and unclenched his fists, ran his fingers through his hair. "I don't *need* this. Civil papers.

Civil! Civil, not criminal, civil! Why am I dealing with criminals?! Three bucks a paper, and now I'm afraid to walk down the street. You know, I've seen that fuckin' Roadrunner around here sometimes. I think he's got a buddy or an old lady in the neighborhood." He leaned against the door behind him, contracted his face and torso, and gave a loud, gravelly groan.

Terry responded: "You are now a bad-ass. Let's celebrate. You like Marty Balin. I think he's singin' at Key #3 tonight."

10

Marty aimed the Smith & Wesson Centennial at one of Terry's paintings. "I really appreciate your comin' out here, and it's a really nice piece. You want another beer, man? But I can't hit nothin' with a two-inch thirty-eight. And this one's hammerless. I want to be able to pull back the hammer so those dudes hear the click."

The tall African-American in the white suit accepted the second beer from Terry. Roger, another one of Ellen's servers, had heard about Marty's run-in with the Key #3 manager and offered to get him an unregistered gun. "Marty, buddy, I'm six-four, two-thirty, ex-Cal taekwondo varsity. Those assholes wouldn't mess with me. But you, man . . . Shit, you got balls takin' this as far as you did. Fuckin' wannabe bikers."

Marty handed the thirty-eight to Roger, who wrapped it in a clean, blue-gray cloth. He pulled a shiny, silver-colored automatic from his Puma athletic bag.

Marty ejected the magazine and jacked the twenty-five caliber round out of the chamber. The slide felt flimsy, almost like one of the beer cans. He again aimed at Terry's painting, then handed it back. Roger scooped up the single round, replaced it in the magazine, inserted the magazine into the pistol, wrapped it in a white terry-cloth hand towel, and put it back into his bag. He wanted to make a sale, but he also wanted to help the younger process server. "Marty, man, this ain't a gun shop. You can't be so choosy. You want a good piece, it's that thirty-eight sittin' in my bag. You know I wouldn't cheat you. If I wanted to cheat people, I wouldn't be workin' for

Ellen. I get guns for ladies and guys who need 'em. You didn't come whinin' to me. I came to you. Marty, these guys are hoods, and they know what you look like. You take that thirty-eight and two hundred rounds and give me two hundred dollars now and another two hundred dollars next week, or whenever you can get it. I know you're good for it. Buy that piece, and start practicing, tomorrow."

And that's what Marty did. He knew the two—Italian or German—small automatic pistols he wanted, but he didn't want to buy a registered gun. If he shot someone, he didn't want to end up in jail and in court, explaining why he was carrying a concealed weapon and shooting someone with it.

He slid the magazine into the butt of the Mauser and stuck the stubby pistol into his waistband, between his left hip and his crotch. He threw on an old, black suit jacket, covering the automatic. Marty heard the low bubble of the choppers' engines as he went out the door.

Two guys were coming up the outside staircase towards him. They were huge—long black hair and beards, sunglasses, leather vests, tattooed forearms. They rapped truncated pool cues on the concrete steps and the railing. They drawled incoherently, like a cross between Kristofferson and the little girl in *The Exorcist*.

Marty turned from the bikers and flew over the railing. Marty's leap went on and on. What happened to gravity? Over his shoulder, the bikers continued to drawl horribly.

The asphalt in front of his Camaro hit his chest and face. No pain. Marty took one step and fell on his face. He took another step and fell on his face. Marty thought: "I'm drunk. But I didn't drink nothin'. I gotta move. They'll kill me. They'll beat me into the driveway. I'll be a stain. Oh, God, help."

Marty rolled over. The Mauser and his hand appeared between his eyes and the hideously drawling thugs. They were ten feet away. "No, man. I'm scared-a-you." They rushed at him but covered no ground.

Marty pulled the trigger and said, "Pow! Pow!" The pistol didn't fire. "I guess the safety's on. Or the Mauser isn't double-action on the first shot. I shoulda' jacked a round into the chamber first. Now they'll be mad at me. I pulled a gun on them."

The bikers hit him with their pool cues. He felt nothing. They jumped up and down on him. Marty felt a couple sharp pains in his stomach and bladder. He saw the beating from his living room window. Then slow-motion instant-replay.

Donny's black Roadrunner was parked next to the Camaro. Donny and his buddy got out and approached Marty's body. Marty looked up from the driveway. Donny smiled, threw a subpoena into Marty's face, and spit on him. The friend said, "You better not come around again."

Marty awoke with a gasp. He turned on the lamp next to his bed and pulled the thirty-eight from the drawer in his night table. He checked the cylinder—loaded, five rounds. No safety. No cocking. Good that he bought a revolver. Just pull the trigger, and it'll go off. He'd try it out at the Chabot Gun Club tomorrow, Saturday.

Monday morning Marty tucked the thirty-eight into the waistband of his jeans between his left hip and his crotch. Things had gone just as he'd anticipated at the range. At fifty yards, none of twenty rounds had landed on the paper target. At twenty-five yards, he'd hit the target with one out of thirty shots. There had been no target set at the appropriate range for the Centennial, less than ten yards. It was an Airweight, and it only fired double-action, so it was even less accurate than a regular two-inch thirty-eight. He thought, "That's OK. I'm not an assassin." The recoil for the aluminum-framed pistol had been stronger than that of a regular thirty-eight, but tolerable. Fun, like firecrackers.

He threw his old black suit jacket on, concealing his piece. Stepping out the door, Marty instantly felt ridiculous. Bright sunshine, his landlord waving hello, the waitress who lived downstairs shouting a greeting. Nine-year-old David from next door asked him if Terry were still around. Terry had befriended the kid, often left alone by his mother. Scary neighborhood. Combat zone.

Slipping in behind the wheel, Marty felt only slight discomfort, but the gun was visible. The suit jacket wouldn't stay forward enough. There were no buttons left. He started the engine, then shut it off immediately, even before turning on the radio. He had forgotten his lunch. Before leaving the apartment the second time, he slipped the thirty-eight into a big, padded envelope, along with the Baggie that contained the peanut butter and jam sandwich he'd made the night before. Returning to the car, he wedged the padded envelope between the driver's seat and the carpeted lump that separated it from the passenger's seat. The way he cornered, he couldn't afford to leave it on the passenger's seat or on the floor. The revolver and the sandwich would have gotten spilled onto the floor. Marty felt a little better with his gun in the padded envelope.

About 1 PM Marty pulled into a MacDonald's in Berkeley, just past Oakland, on Telegraph Avenue. He needed a drink to go with his sandwich. Then, a customer, he'd eat in his car in the MacDonald's parking lot. When Officer Bruce Bernstein walked in, Marty started to feel cold. The process server and the cop immediately recognized each other. "Don't look away," Marty told himself. He looked at the cop and threw him an ironic half-smile. But he started to shake. Forgetting his sandwich, he ordered a Big Mac and a Coke. "Oh, no, he thought, "I already got a sandwich in the car. Yeah, and I also got a year in state prison in the car." He gave the clerk a couple bills and started to give her exact change, but he was shaking. Was she looking at him as if he were an alien or a downed North Vietnamese pilot? He gave up on the exact change and gave her another bill. She gave him the food, and he headed for an outside table. He bumped into Officer Bernstein, stepping on both his feet.

"Got something to be nervous about, Klein?"

"Yeah, Officer. Got a minute?" Marty led Bruce Bernstein out into the parking lot, but far from his Camaro. He leaned against an Impala and said, "Couple guys from Key #3 tried to take me into an alley, and I'm scared shit." He hugged himself, looked at the asphalt, and shook. "What the fuck am I gonna do? Complain to you? You know what I did to almost get sent to a hospital? Same thing I did to you. My job! My thing. It's gettin' to me, Bruce. Up to now I been a pretty sheltered kid, but now I'm scared, man. Just lemme eat my fuckin' lunch, OK? Gimme a business card, and I'll call and tell you the whole story, if you're interested."

Marty accepted the cop's business card and later added it to his stack. He never phoned the cop. The next day he returned the thirty-eight to Roger and got back half of his hundred-dollar deposit. They were cool.

11

MARTY LEANED AGAINST THE wall and watched the fish in the six-foot tank across from Rick's desk. Rick's explanation to an attorney came to him over his shoulder: "Yes, ma'am. . . . Yes, I realize that, ma'am. I know that we should have had him served last week, but . . . You know, ma'am, we're not permitted to enter a private residence, and if he refuses to come to the door, we can't serve him. Now, if you're willing to authorize a stake-out at the home address or the business address, we . . . Yes, ma'am. I'm sorry, ma'am. We'll try to do better. . . . Thank you, ma'am. You have a nice day, too." Rick slammed down the phone. "Fucking moron!"

Marty responded, "Fuckin' A," and accepted a stack of summonses and subpoenas from Rick. He sorted them geographically—first Oakland, then Berkeley—in his car and set off. He found his last target about 6 PM in her back yard. "I guess she's a juicer," thought Marty. Nola Moore stood in the crabgrass behind the run-down home address. She leaned on a shopping cart filled with clothes, a dusty clock radio, and an opened box of crackers. Atop her other belongings sat three sixteen-ounce cans of Colt .45, still in the plastic holder. The fourth can lay empty on the ground. Nola brought the fifth can up to her red, puffy face as she sized up Marty. She looked about forty-five. "Where's the sixth can?" thought Marty. Then he thought, "Here I am, Sherlock Holmes in Berkeley—the *sixth can*."

"Nola Moore?"

"Yeah." She removed her sunglasses to see Marty better. "Who are you?"

"I have some legal papers for you."

"No. Who are you? Who sent you? How did you find me? You're wrong. They're not for me." She backed away.

Marty thought: "No. They're for *me*. They're for Henry Kissinger." He slipped the summons between two of the cans of Colt .45 joined by the plastic holder.

Back in the car, across the street, Marty looked into the yard after doing his paperwork for his last serve of the day. Nola was poring over the document with the eleven-year-old boy who'd been at her side during the serve. Marty pulled a hard half-smile. "Poor kid," he said softly. "And the next one," he thought. Nola was pregnant.

12

"Pastor Deidre's just concerned about us. She told me she really respects you, and she says I should be thankful you've been so generous, poured yourself out for me. She wants to counsel us on the growth of our relationship, and I want you to meet with her and me on Thursday morning."

During Marty's days with the community he sometimes had not seen eye-to-eye with Reverend Deirdre Owen. He did not want her influencing his girlfriend. But Molly wanted him to meet with Deirdre, so he'd take his medicine.

Marty remembered when Pastor Deidre had found out he was planning to hunt wild boar. She had told him that she hoped the wild boars would get him. Marty hadn't reacted, but he'd been impressed. A pacifist divinity graduate wanted wild boars to rip him apart? They weren't even endangered. Wild boar were doing great, across the USA and internationally. After this he'd considered Pastor Deidre Owen a pseudo-pacifist Sierra Club *freak*. Independent of Reverend Owen's curse, he'd given up hunting long before seeing a boar. He rejected a sport whose goal is a suffering animal.

Marty, Molly, and Pastor Deidre met in the pastor's second-floor apartment on a quiet street one block from the Berkeley Police station, sitting under hanging ferns and sipping peppermint tea. Deirdre sat in a cane chair across the coffee table from the couple. An embroidered dove and a feminist fist button adorned her overalls. Her chalky face was dotted with freckles. Behind her wire-rimmed glasses with photo-gray lenses, identical to Marty's, one hazel iris had an imperfection, a jagged black area that ran from the white to the pupil. Marty had always wondered if this impaired her vision. Deirdre's blonde hair was cut shorter than Marty's, in the style of a Midwestern gym teacher, a Berkeley feminist, or Camilla Hall of the Symbionese Liberation Army. As Deirdre counseled, she coughed and ate a hard-boiled egg. Never in robust health, she followed a strict diet.

The pastor leaned forward, rubbed her hands down and up the tops of her thighs, and gulped air. "Marty, it's good to see you again. I've missed you since you left the community. You're real special, and we've all missed your special contribution to the Body of Christ. You seem tense. Do you have any negative feelings or fears about our meeting? I'm not here to judge you. I'm going to help you and Molly with your relationship."

"Uhh ... yeah ... uh," Marty started, "I fear you don't approve of me or anything I'm into. You don't want Molly mixed up with me, and you're a strong influence on her."

"Marty, that's not true. You're a good brother. You were so good with the street people."

Marty thought, "Save it, Deirdre."

"You've become harder since you left the community, Marty. That concerns me. Molly's told me about your job. Don't you realize you're serving the world's system, oppressing the poor?"

"I serve papers on everybody: the rich, the poor, government, businesses, the University. Serving people notifies them of their trials. Serving people with legal papers is part of the American system. How'd you like to be tried in your absence?"

"The American system is opposed to the kingdom of God. Christians must find a creative alternative. You are now a member of a church that has chaplains in the Army, that had chaplains in the Nazi army! Can't you understand that a church that does not stand against the genocide of the Jewish people or the Vietnamese people is a stench in the nostrils of God?!"

"No, Deirdre."

"The German Lutheran Church doesn't ordain women. Molly is an intelligent, gifted counselor, a servant of Christ. She and I could not be ordained in your Lutheran Church. How do you think that makes her feel? Do you like that discriminatory policy, Molly?"

Molly started to answer, "No, but I . . ."

Deirdre continued, "Marty, you use the racist epithet 'gook.' I've heard you use it casually, callously. How do you think that makes Molly feel?"

"She knows I'm not a bigot. Usually I say 'gook' in the context of the war."

"To denigrate patriots fighting against American imperialism!"

"Something like that."

"Marty, you were a good brother. You've become a bitter young man. How do you think that makes me feel?"

"Bitter?"

Molly smothered a laugh. Pastor Deirdre shot her a hard look and turned to Marty. "You think this is funny?! You're going to need a lot of help before you can have a healthy, Godly relationship. First, you've got to leave that lukewarm establishment church and get back into community. Then you've got to find a creative alternative to your participation in the system of racist imperialism that is euphemistically called the American system of justice. *And* I'm going to have to start counseling you one-on-one, Marty. You've got to get your head together. Then *we'll see* about a relationship between you two. Right now there's no point in my talking to you together."

13

MARTY AND MOLLY DRANK their coffee at the Berkeley McDonald's. She told him: "Marty, it'll be OK. Don't worry. I love you. Marty, look at me." He watched the passersby and kept an eye on his filthy white Camaro. He grunted, made a couple pleasant responses, drank his coffee, and dropped her off at Durant House with a forced smile and a promise to call the next day.

After work on Friday Marty called the Durant House pay phone. Molly answered—too up, too animated, nervous. The process server offered to buy her dinner at Pik's.

"Marty, I'd love to, but I can't. Remember what Pastor Deirdre said yesterday? Well. Well. Well. She told me last night she doesn't want me seeing you anymore. She says you're too different."

"You know that's not true. Didn't you tell her that?"

"Yes," Molly said evenly. "I told her you were dear to me. But she disagreed. She said it wouldn't do either of us any good. You're a German Lutheran, and you're not going to change."

"I've been a good boyfriend. I take my medicine when I have to."

"You're the best, Marty. Your description doesn't do you justice." She pressed her lips together and looked up at the ceiling. "But . . . "

"Molly, please. Our love is like a nice little animal, a poor little animal. Please don't let it die."

Molly swallowed, took a deep breath, and spoke slowly. "But Pastor Deirdre is my spiritual authority, and she's responsible for me. She's already thought and prayed about this. She's *decided*. I have an idea, Marty: make believe I died. I have to go now, Marty. Good-by."

www.ingramcontent.com/pod-product-compliance
Lightning Source LLC
Chambersburg PA
CBHW071227170626
46809CB00005BA/1965